THE LEGEND OF MORVIDUS: LORD OF WARWICKSHIRE

THE BEAR, THE BAT AND THE RAGGED STAFF

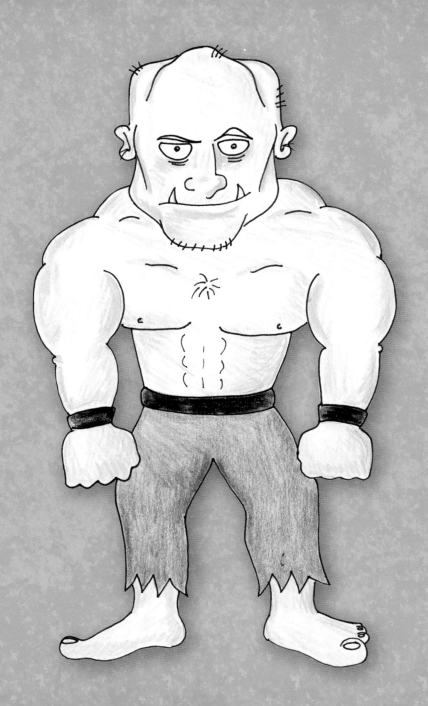

THE LEGEND OF MORVIDUS: LORD OF WARWICKSHIRE

THE BEAR, THE BAT AND THE RAGGED STAFF

Written by Rachael Wong

Illustrated by Jim Troughton

BREWIN BOOKS

First published by
Brewin Books Ltd, 56 Alcester Road,
Studley, Warwickshire B80 7LG in 2015

www.brewinbooks.com

ISBN: 978-1-85858-538-3

A Cataloguing in Publication Record
for this title is available from the British Library.

Typeset in Jerky Tash.
Printed in Great Britain by
Cambrian Printers.

All over the world,

Wherever they play,

Stars of tomorrow

Are starting today.

All royalties from this book will be given directly to the

Warwickshire Cricket Board to support youth cricket

projects at all age groups and levels.

To become a Friend of Warwickshire Youth Cricket visit:

www.warwickshirecricketboard.co.uk

For Bellie and Buster - RW

For Naomi, Eva and Rosie - JT

FOREWORD

"Having worn a Warwickshire shirt all these years, through the age groups and up to the first team, I have always been intrigued about the origin of the bear and the ragged staff on our badge. The legend of Morvidus is the root of the courage, strength and determination embedded in that badge and this story will be loved by all Bears, young and old. Past club captain, and my good friend, Jim Troughton has shown yet again what a talented man he is with his wonderful illustrations. They bring Morvidus to life and capture a special time in anyone's childhood – their first cricket match."

Ian Bell MBE, Warwickshire & England

"And that is the story of how brave Morvidus fought the giant and brought peace to Warwickshire," said the lady who was showing Alex's class around the old castle.

"I hope you have all enjoyed your day with us here, but now it is time for you to go home."

Alex smiled at Mum. He had enjoyed the school trip and liked it when Mum came to help. She always told really good stories on the bus.

That evening, when he got home, Alex packed his new cricket bag very carefully. He put it next to the front door, ready for the morning.

Tomorrow, Alex would be playing in his first ever cricket match, for his local club. He knew he had to make sure he had packed everything he needed.

"Pads, helmet, gloves?" asked Dad.

Alex nodded.

"And your bat, of course," added Dad.

"Of course, Dad," replied Alex.

Alex walked slowly up the stairs to get ready for bed. Although he was very excited about playing in his first match, he was also quite nervous. His coach, Tom, had said everyone would get a turn to bat and bowl in the match.

Alex had been to watch lots of cricket matches. His sister, Izzy, played for one of the Warwickshire girls' teams and he liked going to watch her. Izzy bowled VERY fast. Alex loved the way her hair flew out behind her as she stormed in to bowl. Sometimes you couldn't even see the ball when she bowled it! All you saw were the bails flying through the air and the girl who was batting would then walk back to her team looking really disappointed.

Mum was folding up the clean washing on the landing.

"What's up?" she asked, as Alex came up the stairs.

"I'm a bit nervous about tomorrow, Mum," replied Alex. "Tom says it will be a game of pairs cricket; so we all bat and bowl. I like bowling, and Tom says I bowl straight, but I'm very worried about batting. What happens if someone bowls really fast at me, like Izzy does? What if I can't even see the ball and I'm out before I know it? Or, what if the ball hits me and hurts me?"

Mum smiled. "Remember the story the lady at the castle told us today about brave Morvidus?"

Alex nodded.

Mum sat down at the top of the stairs. "Shall I tell it to you again?" she asked. "I think it will make you feel more confident about your match tomorrow."

"Yes please," said Alex, and he settled down next to Mum on the stairs to listen.

"Brave Morvidus was the Lord of Warwickshire a long time ago. He was said to be as brave and strong as a bear. In fact, one of his friends even gave him a special wooden shield with a picture of a bear carved into it.

One day, Morvidus was riding through the forest to visit his friend. He kept a watchful eye on the forest as there were stories in the villages of evil monsters and giants who came out of the trees to harm people.

Suddenly, Morvidus heard a noise close by in the bushes. Then there was a blood-chilling howl and Morvidus saw an angry looking giant come running out of the forest towards him.

The giant was twice as tall as Morvidus. He was completely bald and had wild staring eyes. His teeth were as sharp as knives and his hands were as big as shovels.

Before Morvidus knew what was happening, the giant knocked him off his horse and he fell to the ground, banging his head on a tree. Morvidus managed to keep hold of his shield, but his sword was lost in the bushes.

Morvidus needed a weapon and he needed it quickly, before the giant struck again. He felt the carving of the bear on his shield and suddenly it filled him with the strength and courage of a bear.

In a flash, Morvidus was up on his feet. The giant was almost upon him. Morvidus spun around and smashed his shield into the oncoming monster. The giant reeled and, in an instant, Morvidus reached behind him and pulled on the tree he had fallen against. Such was his new strength, the tree came clean out of the ground.

While the giant struggled to his feet, Morvidus quickly stripped the branches off the tree and turned to face his enemy, holding the tree before him like a staff.

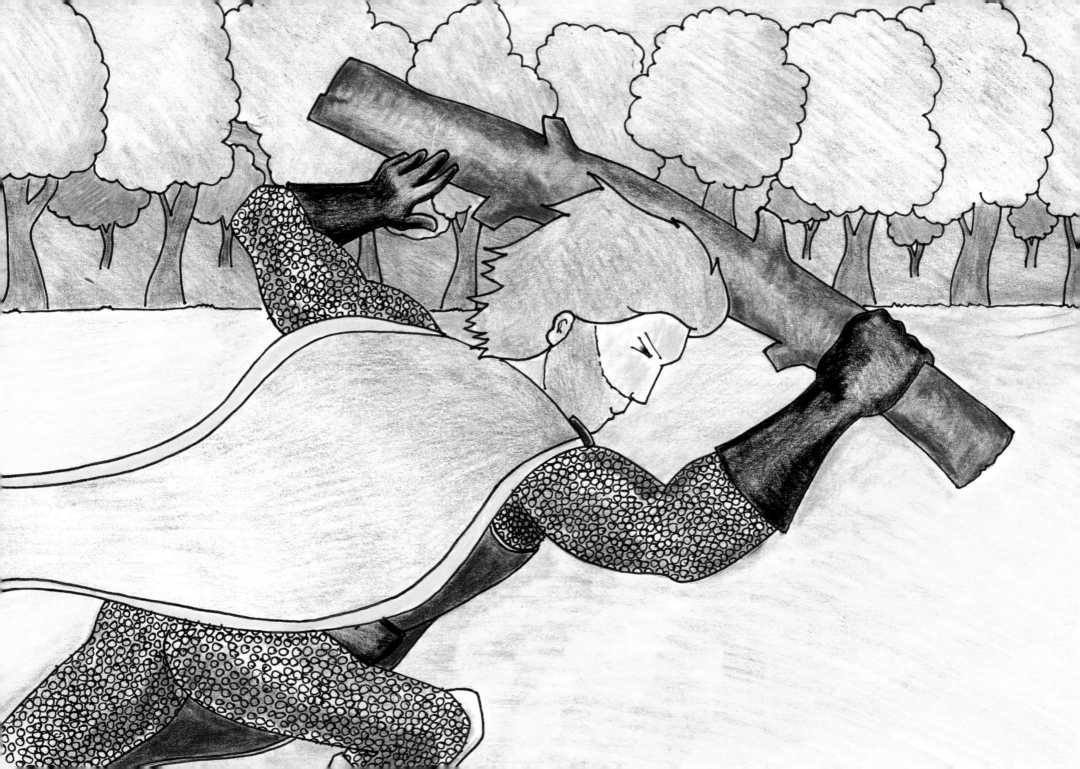

As the giant approached, Morvidus swung his staff with such might that it knocked the giant clean off his feet. The giant was so large, and he hit the ground so hard, that all the trees in the forest shook.

Morvidus stood over the giant and said, 'Enough! Go back into the forest and never trouble me or my people again.'

The giant looked up at Morvidus and realised he was beaten. He crawled back into the forest and was never seen again.

Once the giant had disappeared into the forest, Morvidus let out a huge sigh of relief. He realised how lucky he was to have beaten the giant, especially having lost his sword. Morvidus leaned against the raggedy staff and marvelled how his bear shield had given him the strength to uproot that tree and use it to defeat the giant.

It only took Morvidus a few minutes to find his lost sword in the bushes, and then he saw his horse, waiting patiently for him further along the path. 'I have had good fortune today,' said Morvidus to himself.

Morvidus continued his journey to his friend's village. When he arrived and told his story, there was a big feast in celebration of the defeat of the giant. Some of the men in the village went into the forest and brought back the raggedy staff Morvidus had used. It was put up in the village and the children danced around it.

Before Morvidus returned home, he had the shape of the raggedy staff carved on his shield alongside the bear.

For many years, thanks to Morvidus, there was peace in the land and the people lived well. The bear and the raggedy staff lived on as a symbol of strength and courage, long after Morvidus.

And so," said Mum, finishing the story, "Tomorrow when you walk out to bat, try to imagine you are like brave Morvidus. Believe you are as brave and strong as a bear, and that your bat is your raggedy staff."

"If you can do that," continued Mum, "I am sure you will be absolutely fine. Remember, whatever happens, we will all be really proud of you."

The next day, the match started and Alex's team batted first. The other team had an enormous bowler who bowled almost as fast as Izzy. Alex's team-mates were soon bowled or caught out and stomped grumpily back to the boundary afterwards. Alex waited with his friend Farhad for their turn to bat.

"Alex and Farhad," said Tom eventually, "It's your turn now. We need a few runs here, boys, so do the best you can."

"Just like brave Morvidus," thought Alex as he walked out towards the crease. He held his head high and his bat really tightly.

In a few moments, the first ball came towards him. Alex could see it clearly, and he knew exactly what to do with it…